Freezy Breezy Fun

By Allan Poulsen
Illustrated by Kim Raymond

 A GOLDEN BOOK • NEW YORK

Golden Books Publishing Company, Inc., New York, New York 10106

Library of Congress Catalog Card Number: 99-67692   ISBN: 0-307-12891-1   A MM   First Edition 2000

One morning Pooh woke up and felt that something was different. The Hundred-Acre Wood was very quiet. It was as if everything outside were wrapped in cotton . . .

or snow!

Pooh jumped out of bed and ran to the window. What a sight! There was thick white snow as far as he could see.

"Oh, my!" Pooh said out loud. "All that snow fell in one night. And I didn't even hear it falling. I must go tell Piglet in case he hasn't seen it yet."

Pooh hurried to find his sled and his warmest scarf.

Knock! Knock! Pooh knocked on Piglet's door,
but there was no answer.

"I bet he's still sleeping," Pooh said to himself.

"Piglet! Piglet!" Pooh called. "It's time to wake up and play in the snow."

After a little while a sleepy Piglet opened the door. "W-w-why are you y-y-yelling, Pooh?" Piglet said as he shivered from the cold.

"Look at all the snow!" Pooh shouted excitedly. "Let's go sledding!"

Piglet got dressed, put on his scarf, and was ready to go. Pooh pulled Piglet on the sled as they headed toward their favorite hill.

"Thanks for the ride, Pooh," said Piglet. "Little feet are not made for deep snow."

All of a sudden, Tigger came bounding toward them. "Isn't it a beautiful day?" he said. Tigger then bounced a great big bounce and slid to a stop, covering Piglet with a cold white mound of snow.

That gave Pooh an idea. "Let's have a
contest to see who can make the biggest
and best snowman in the Hundred-Acre
Wood!" he said.

"Sounds like fun!" agreed Tigger.

"G-g-get me out of this snow," was all
Piglet could say.

Pooh, Tigger, and Piglet went to tell Roo, Rabbit, and Eeyore, and soon they were all ready to start the contest. They each did their best, but they discovered that on their own it was hard to make a snowman.

"Let's work together," suggested Pooh. "Together we can make an even bigger and better snowman!"

"But then no one will win the contest," said Tigger.

"If we make the biggest and best snowman ever seen, then we'll all be winners," Rabbit explained.

Working together, Pooh, Tigger, and Piglet rolled an extra large ball of snow. At the same time, Eeyore, Rabbit, and Roo rolled a medium-sized snowball.

After they lifted the smaller snowball on top of the larger one, they stepped back to admire their work. It was a very big snowman, but something was missing.

"I know!" Roo said excitedly. "Our snowman needs a scarf to stay warm. He can wear mine."

Eeyore gave Roo a boost so he could put his scarf around the snowman's neck. It looked great. Eeyore stayed with Roo as the others hurried to their homes to get more items for the snowman to wear.

"Don't you want to get something for the snowman?" Roo asked Eeyore.

"I already have what the snowman needs," Eeyore said. "My tail. Every snowman should have a tail."

When everyone returned, each showed off what he had brought for the snowman. Rabbit brought a carrot to make the perfect nose.

Pooh brought a pot of honey, because even a snowman has a tummy to fill!

Piglet brought a top hat just the right size for a large snowman.

And Tigger brought sunglasses, because he thought they would make the snowman look extraspecially tiggerific.

Finally the snowman was complete. He was the biggest,
best-looking snowman the Hundred-Acre Wood had ever seen!

After all that hard work, everyone was hungry.
So the friends went to Piglet's house for a snack.
   "I think we did a great job," said Rabbit.
   "Yes," agreed Roo, "it's the best snowman in
the whole world!"

"You know what I like best about the snow?" Pooh asked. "Getting to warm up inside with hot chocolate, honey, and good friends."

"Me, too," agreed Roo. "But after we warm up, let's go back outside. We can have a lot more fun in the snow!"

WINTER FUN

Here are some great ways for you and your friends to have lots of snowy winter fun, just like Pooh and his pals. Be sure to ask an adult before you try any of these crafts and activities.

MAKE TINY SNOWPEOPLE

Instead of making one big snowman, you and your friends can make a whole family of small ones. Little sticks or twigs can be used for arms or even hair. And pebbles or raisins make good eyes.

Don't stop with the family members. Your tiny snowpeople will want a little snow car or sled, a snow pet, and even a snow house. What's really great about tiny snowpeople is that you can bring them home with you. Clear a space in the freezer so you can visit your snow family whenever you like!

BUILD WITH SNOW

Bring plastic pails, buckets, or food containers outside on a snowy day. Fill the containers with snow, turn them upside down, and gently lift them up. You've got instant snow buildings! The snow shapes can even be placed one on top of the other to create forts and castles!

MAKE A BIRD FEEDER

It can be hard for birds to find food during the winter. If you make this bird feeder, your feathered friends will know where to go for a good meal.

Ask an adult to cut out the sides of an empty milk carton as shown in the illustration. Punch a hole in the top and thread heavy string or wire through it. You can decorate the outside of the feeder with paint, and glue leaves and sticks to it. Be sure to use a glue that will hold up in the rain and snow.

When the paint and glue have dried, bring the feeder outside and hang it from a sturdy tree branch. Fill the bottom of the feeder with birdseed or bread crumbs and watch to see who comes to eat.

Remember to fill the feeder with food all winter. The birds will continue to come back, and you don't want to disappoint them or have them go hungry!

PLAY CATCH THE SNOWBALL

Take a sheet of heavy card stock and tape it together to form a cone shape, as shown. Then crumple up a piece of white writing paper. This is your snowball. Tie a 12-inch piece of string to the snowball and attach the other end of the string to the cone as shown below.

To play, hold the cone in one hand with the pointed end facing down. Then swing the snowball in the air and try to catch it inside the cone.

MAKE HOT CHOCOLATE

Drinking hot chocolate is a perfect way to warm up. And preparing it can be fun, too!

Ask an adult to make a pot of hot chocolate and pour it into some mugs. Then you can add big clumps of whipped cream on top. Decorate the cream with chocolate chips or brightly colored candy. Try making a whipped-cream face, or other silly designs.

WATCH IT SNOW

Find an empty glass jar or a clear plastic container that has a lid. Create a scene in the jar by gluing small plastic toys, stones, and twigs inside of it. Make sure to use a glue that will work underwater.

When the glue is dry, fill the jar with water until it is almost full. Then pour a small handful of glitter inside. Close the lid tightly. When you turn your jar upside down and then right-side up again, you can watch it snow inside!